Do You Have Some Time to Spare?

Augusto Iglesias

to my family for supporting me through thick and thin

Table of Content

"Express yourself they say. What's the point? Freud believed that if you talked enough about what was going on to you that you would feel better. Guess that's what I'm attempting here? But what does it mean to "express myself"? If I do not know who I am or what I am expressing? Should I talk about what I would like to be, my struggles, my day, what I like, etc? What should I write here? Will it even work? Worth a shot I guess. After all, I like writing and need an outlet. What should I express? What does it mean to express? Google says: to convey (a thought or feeling) in words or by gestures and conduct. So if I want to express myself that means I have to convey my thoughts and feelings here. On this page. This blank page. Total freedom to write whatever and I choose to write about myself to feel better about myself. Is that selfish? Maybe a better word is egocentric? I don't know. Maybe that's what I need to do to solve issues. Consider myself before others. Love myself before I love others. Im guessing my ego is low, so to boost it up I have to write about myself, for myself, to myself. I, I, I. Me, myself and I. Am I that great? Are my feelings worth writing down? I am positive someone else could do this better than me. Oh well. I said I would give it a shot, so I should. It can't hurt. Who am I? As an entity in this planet what is my identity? I feel like I identify myself as an unknown. So I guess that means I have to express nothing? Or mystery? I am done." -my soul reasoning.

Introduction of my *stuff*:

Thanks for your time. I do not deserve it. I am no one to you and who I am should not matter either. All that matters are these words and what I decide to do with them. Want to see what I do? If so, then read on.

I must warn you though, to keep on reading means you must have an objective, yet open mind towards the essence of this reading.

I hope you can cope.

"What is the essence of this reading?", you may wonder. Well, let me respond by saying that it is a collection of *stuff* I have written throughout my life. Each *stuff* I wrote is connected to a certain moment and time of my life. Some of the *stuff* will be good, some of the *stuff* will be bad. Since I am no one to you, I hope to make up for it with my *stuff*. Judge at the end.

Judge me right and know that the essence of this reading, for me, is not me. Maybe I am more or less. You will never know, for you are not me.

Overall, this collection will touch on various themes. All I hope is for anyone that is willing to read all this *stuff* to the end, to find a piece of themselves here.

I hope you enjoy the *stuff*!

Section 1: Passion

Passion is what encourages your desires. Passion can either drive you to punch someone in the face or press your lips on someones face.

The Purity in the Madness

I was lost in the dark streets. The sidewalk was wet from piss and vomit, a common sign of nightlife, it had not rained in days. All of the laughter and screaming came from the bars and reached my ears as swiftly a melody can. I went in to see these people's temples of the impaired. I found a satisfying numbness from the chaos that was radiated by these distorted, sweaty faces. All of their existence left open in front of these dark streets. I was seduced by the treacheries of the men behind the bar and the women behind the make up. I was in a coma of indifference to anything that could happen. I was now lost in this world of distracting pleasures, the pleasures being the distractions themselves. In this place, I would interact by trying to push others off the edge. I chose to misplace others comfortability, in exchange for their insanity. With just words, I ventured out to dissociate even further the minds of those who were willing to show their candid self and allow it to be liberated onto me. I became the chaos that freed. I was told that I was intense. It is just passion. Passion for the purity in the madness.

I Want the World

I want to make her cry because she likes it too much.

I want to make her scream so loud that she has to cover her mouth.

I want to make her feel the climax I impose take control of her mind.

I want to get her body to move in such a way that it begs for more, more and more.

I want to make every inch of her tender body shiver.

I want to make her eyes roll back in such a way that says, "I am done".

I want to have her wish for my breaking and weakening.

I want to birth, kill and resuscitate her in just one act.

I want her to praise me like a God, so she will let me rule as one.

What I Felt We Felt

We sat at the couch and started talking. We were having a few drinks as we talked. We did not have many drinks, just enough to make us loose. A good kind of loose, the kind of loose that comes along with a bold opening. We started to laugh at each other more, touch each other more, look at each other more. We did everything with each other more and we felt more than fine doing it. We both knew this, so we got closer. We were so close that we felt the warmth of each others skin radiating. Our hearts uncontrollably bouncing inside of our chest because of the proximity. Our brain's exotic imagination stopping us from connecting our eyes path. We did not look at each other. Our faces were pointed down as if bowing towards each others souls. After a few suspenseful moments passed, we looked up. We made our eyes wrinkle, but our smile crinkle. Her lips were soft. My lips were wet. Her skin was rubbed. My skin was hot. Her shirt was off. My shirt was on the floor. Her arms were a halo. My arms were an arch. We were not a good match.

A Mental Break Down Going Down on a Break Up

I can't write if the room is too bright. So I get up and turn off the light. I don't know if you can tell, but I don't feel quite well. My stomach is a knot tied real tight. I feel like a kite uncontrollably taking flight, my eyes looking for someone to fight, while my teeth cry for something hard to bite. I try to recite those words that keep me alright, but I remember I made you sad that night. And that makes me mad tonight. And now I'm up all night. You see, my height is 6'2. But just because I'm big, don't mean I don't feel blue about how I broke up with you. Even if it was true, tonight I'm going cuckoo. I'm trying to express how I feel because lately I've been feeling ill. No one knows since I pretend to be made out of steel, so no one can reveal what is under this hard peel. And when I explode I unseal everything I am trying to conceal. I try to hide it all by saying "it's no big deal". I'm wondering if you fucked someone. I'm wondering if you thought it was fun. I'm wondering if you are calling him hun and if he made you smile bright like the sun, like I use to do and I sure as hell hope its not better than what I use to do. I'm wondering if he is calling you boo. I'm wondering if he makes you feel good. I'm wondering if he makes you shout "oo!" and makes you feel brand new. Maybe I shouldn't of broken up with you. Boo-hoo. I miss you. I don't miss you. I want you. I don't want you. I need you. I don't need you. I love you. I don't love you. The only thing I know, is I don't know and that things weren't okay. And yeah you would call me bae, but we were destined to decay. Doomsday was at our doorway and we tried to say we were A-Okay, but what lay beyond all that foul play and past that gate was that day where we were Doomsday's bate. We didn't know whether to love or to hate. You know what day Im talking about... The day you and I said goodbye. Whose fault is it? Probably the both of us? We could play the blame game, but I don't want any fame or to call out your name or name after name. I don't want to point fingers. I don't want to cry and fight. I am just looking for closure and this poem was my big exposure. I am sure many things will change about how I feel, but I know in my heart you will be kept sealed. I know it's over between us two. And it should stay like that too. So my last words to you, like Timon, Pumbaa and Simba: Good night. Sleep tight. Don't let the bed bugs bite.

Love as Destruction

She destroys when she loves.
He lets what he loves destroy him.
She hates to love and love hates him.
They both let love destroy them.
And that to them is love.

Making Love

What's the point of fucking,
if you don't fuck
her good?

What a Pretty Nothing

Oh prince charming arouse me
with the emptiness
that is hidden
in your delicate white hands.

Slaughter Me, Eat Me
Cut my throat
with your clit
and put pressure
with you lips.

Cannibalism
Fuck your heart,
give me your skin.

The Things I Am Used Too

I was in
shock,
but
comfortable.

Conforming to Try Hard

I don't care what you give me
life,
just let me fuck the shit out of
it!

Section 2: Freestyle

What I do when I feel something chaotic, but there is too much chaos to organize any of it.

What I Am in the AM

I write best between three AM and four AM, probably because it's when my subconscious starts to creep its way into my conscience hands that tippity tip tap on the keyboard of my iPhone touch screen.

I am deciding to put in neat fashion my wild thoughts of how, right now, I want to be your everything, that is best at everything ever, all the time, past and future, every time, forever and please do not say never ever forever.

Does that make sense? No? Yes? Maybe so?

All I am between the AMs is: I am playing around with words, their sounds, their meaning and their order. This is because I do not want to be formal about how we say former, before stating what we were, in order to make this not so fun thing a fun thing. I did not mean to run on that sentence.

Or did I?

By it is a late night.

Miracle

She lays upon the skin of another believing it is her own. In her utopian reality, she is the king of this blue sphere. This blue sphere is the center of the universe. And she is the center of what is the center of the universe.

She closes her eyes with ease and with a mindset that an optimistic tomorrow awaits her. The chest that moves her head up and down is nothing short of calming.

She is a lady of her imagination. Mystical. With just a glance, she can surge into your subconscious mind and strip you naked of who you believe to be.

She will show you who you really are. Gasp. Be careful. Be cautious. You may not be enough.

She is seen as a goddess in all senses, since in all senses she is harmony.

Aphrodite?

She carries herself with a self fulfilling purpose that reads as a miracle because she is one. Thank you, beauty, that is truly beautiful.

The Eyeballs, the Eyelids and the Soul

Did my eyelids get heavier since the last time I blinked? I can barely open my eyelids. If I keep blinking will my eyelids get so heavy that I won't be able to open them again? Okay. I need tape to keep them open.

The tape is keeping my eyelids open, but now a layer of my eyeballs feel like they are burnt away with some sort of acid. Let me take the tape off.

My eyeballs feel better now. I had to blink for that to happen, which was not an all around good thing because now my eyelids are unbearable to maintain open. My eyelids are twitching due to all the force they are having to withstand. I might break any second now.

I broke. I am typing with my eyes closed now. I don't know how Im doing it, but I am. My fingers know this keyboard like my fingers know the palm of my hand that this keyboard is on. I see nothing. Blackness.

Wait. Wait! I see a face.

What's going on?!

The face I see with my eyes totally closed is beautiful.

Why is it smiling?

I feel something in me. Fireworks in my belly?

Pop. Pop!

This is overwhelming!

I know there is no face and no fireworks, yet I feel them. I feel my body now closing in on this face, my hands on her soft cheeks and my eyelashes passing through hers. Are we kissing?

How is this possible?

I know I am in bed just typing. Yet this feels so real. My eyes feel open, but they are closed? My hands feel as if they aren't on something hard, but rather something soft?

My lips are wet. My mouth is full with a tongue that's not mine and with saliva I don't recognize.

What is happening?

Why are you leaving?

Vanishing in the bright light?

Wait.

My hands are back on the keyboard.

What? Oh.

My head makes a nod, nod, nod.

I don't see a god, god, god.

Rubbery. Rub. Fuck.

Look at my face when it sees the base of your arms extension.

Preliminary hearing to see if I am fleeting out of this world with my head that is not in bed and needs to be fed, by what you think is good, but it is just a rude taste. Now it's all a waste.

It's a fake lake, so take it away because it makes me throw the up to the top lop on a dumb gum.

This makes no sense, since this is my brain on a sharp fence and now my defense is at an all time low. Oh, no.

I am with racks of desires, all forgotten like street flyers.

Eyes jaded and mind faded.

Hands shaky and body achy.

Need that magic potion to put my soul into an absorption. Oh, yes. That numbness can fix my dumbness.

Raggedy dog sees life through a thick fog. Where you walking, dawg? He answers by saying, "I am on a split log going nowhere and I hope for a place somewhere, where there is a fair share of meaning. Right now though, life feels like a big nope and I just smoke dope to not put my neck on a rope or elope":

I answered, "Oh what a sad life, put a knife to my wicked mad head. Am I dead? Where is the instead?".

Why is a mirror opaque and a window transparent?
My window is dirty
and I cant see me looking at
you.

Los Dos Mundos que Criaron a un Chico

Un país donde el aire que respiro entra en mis pulmones y grita desde abajo: "este es mi hogar". Los árboles y sus ramas me saludan. Las calles se doblan como una sonrisa de bienvenida. El cielo y el sol me supervisan como padres.

Un país donde los árboles, las calles, la veredas, los edificios y la gente viven sin vida. Pensamientos fluidos y libres no llegan a la superficie en este lugar. El sol y el cielo parecen ser más distantes, sus caras no se reconocen. La luna y las estrellas son pesadamente tristes. Se pisa el suelo y se siente un hueco en la tierra, ahí las emociones son neutrales. El aire que se respira se siente seco. Huelo la muerte y lo superficial es el motor del país.

Nací en el cielo, para después ser envuelto en líneas del norte.

Prefiero un verano con el sol trayendo felicidad antes que la noche triste.

No Es Nada

Me miro en el espejo.
No me noto en el reflejo.
Que es lo que tengo.
Porque no me encuentro.
Tengo ojos repletos de sangre.
No le digas nada a mi madre.
Solo soy yo el que ve esto.
Nadie mas ve todo esto.

En la calle camino por las estrellas.
Es común, es una noche de aquellas.

No me mires que no te veo.
No me digas que no te creo.
No me toques que no te siento.
No me respires que no te huelo.

El sol se va con las nubes del cielo.
No me gusta, por favor, devolvelo.
Las flores se van con los vientos del invierno.
Y yo sólo en las calles de Palermo.
Los árboles se despiden con sus últimos suspiros.
Me dejan sólo con los malos espíritus.
La muerte que trae el planeta.
Me deja en el alma una grieta.

En la calle camino por las veredas.
Ya se fueron todas las estrellas.
Es común, es una noche de aquellas.

No me mires que no te veo.
No me digas que no te creo.
No me toques que no te siento.
No me respires que no te huelo.

Section 3: Lessons

Things that one can try to imagine, but only few can experience. Things that one try to understand, but only few accept. Things that one can try to apply, but only few can develop.

Ownership versus Control

There is a difference between ownership and control. A sense of ownership is more territorial, rather than manipulative. When one acquires property it is to simply state that this property is theirs and no one else's. It is not to be shared. They must be stamped as the owner and no one may indulge in the properties benefits except for themselves. There is a clear line between who is superior and who is inferior. That line is not to be messed with. However, someone who longs for control is far more methodological and will be sure to make you believe your actions are genuine. He/she does not seek to own you, but to manipulate your soul and corrupt you. The person who seeks for control, seeks to break and reconfigure. He/she can sway the worlds views, while appearing incapable. Someone who is in control makes the other think they are owning, while they shift the gears behind the scenes. The idea of owning someone is merely but a feeling one enjoys to wallow in, the act of control is a toil one must go about with precision. Judge correctly for it is crucial.

Am I a Character?

I have been an actor my whole life and my fans love me.

Or do they?

I meant so much to everyone that I became a classic.

A universal bias?

The actors are forgotten and the characters are the ones who stay.

Who is telling my story?

I did not play the role, the role played me.

Manufactured

Any good machine has integrity. Every piece of it has a purpose and a function. A human can perfectly be described as a machine only if they have a purpose. Otherwise they are just malfunctioning pieces without any real intent. I feel as the latter and loath it. I feel as if these thoughts written on these pages are just pieces of my soul and I have, for some reason not apparent to me, begun to collect them. Am I trying to connect them and make them a part of who I am? No. They are just here on these pages and that's just about it. No meaning. No purpose. Just like life was intended to be. Am I hoping for some sort of virtuous revelation to occur to me? Yes, because this emptiness is killing me and I do not want to die unfulfilled. I want to be a working machine, but I have no gas. Being responsible for one's purpose and happiness is hard. What kind of God creates a machine with freedom?

If You Like to Read This You Need Help

We always look to other things to define us and tell us who we are. The problem with looking out into the world for answers is just that. The answers lie within oneself. You can look out into the world, but to explore is to experience things. To experience something you must be subjective and the introspective thinking that will follow such experience will lead you to find an answer within yourself. When you look at a pretty mountain, the mountain is only pretty through your eyes and no one else's. Learn to think for yourself and find beauty for yourself. Beauty lies within the eyes of the beholder after all. If what I write speaks to you in any way than I hope you can learn to speak for yourself, I shouldn't have to do it for you.

Demigod

We look at what we want to be, but not what we have to do to be that. This is how society has made our heroes. We have managed to grab kids to see a hero fight the evil, but we forget what hell is like. A hero is nothing but a sociopath doing the right thing and praised for it. A hero has sound sleep because others love him, but never for what he does. If a hero finds joy in his accomplishments it is do to the reward, not for himself. A mythical creature. A God, not a human. That's why they have "powers". The anti-hero, however, is a man of much more integrity. The anti-hero is more natural. Although the anti-hero can be seen as the underdog at many times because of his mischievous ways, it can be argued that his flaws make him a far more wholesome being when compared to a hero. A hero is nothing but a dream, so a human's closest shot is an antihero. Tell your kids unless you want them to be burned by the sun. Although a sad realization, it is a necessary evil for those who want to be the "best".

Deception as a Tool

My instructions are what pave
my revolution in
disguise.

Please Stop Them
I hate my burdens,
they seek safety at the expense of
others...
I will kill
them...

You Cannot Take What Is Mine

My trademark is registered to my souls name.
This is authenticity that no one can take.
They would not be able to, even if they tried.

The Duality of Creation

Words are ways for us to express how we
feel,
but words also dictate how we
feel.

The Duality of Mankind

Mean people hate my
kindness,
and kind people are afraid of my hatred.

Do Not Let Shit Get Me
I know that what I did was because I was
sad.
Within those intentions,
I learnt I am
self destructive when
destroyed.

The Duality of Experiences
The most important people
for your growth
give your life the most
painful and lovely
days.

The Help of Diversity
Everyone is looking for happiness,
people just look for it differently.
Can you learn from them?

A Clear Purpose

You can't have anything meaningful with something that has no meaning.

Craziness will always be craziness.

So don't try to understand and just enjoy the fun.

Ignore the irrational and make your own meaning throughout the chaos.

Back When I Was a Spy

You're so good at lying
you can't even tell when
you do it to
yourself.

Las Curas de la Vida

El abrazo medica la melancolía.

Un beso anestesia la ansiedad.

Y el amor, depende de como uno lo use, sana.

Fuck Affection, Let us be Efficient?

Affection is weird, efficiency is not.

Letting go of people could be simple, if it weren't for attachment.

Everyone can be disposed of, the tricky part is finding a replacement.

Sometimes I dispose of people because I needed them for a moment and I do not care if someone disposes of me for the same reasons since I know I will always be fine.

I just hope that those who dispose of me do not regret it.

I want them to be okay.

I guess this is selfish, but most people do not understand me.

So why love me?

Only thing I care about is for my wishes to be satisfied and for those who I care for to want the same.

Am I a Sociopath?

I feel fine.

A Simple Equation
Love+Respect=Peace

Section 4: Numb

What everyone wants when chasing your passion goes from a feeling of accomplishment to a feeling of disaster.

Healthy Drugs

The stream of desensitization coursing through my body.

I think in a jail and wrap my body up.

I am a mummy in all senses.

With a heart that beats from behind the scenes.

I need to wake up and face reality, but fuck that shit.

What are the Point of Memories, if they are Not Reality?

Only thing that remains are the memories and those feelings that came along with them. Those moments are the things I am left with. They give me nostalgia. I look at the old swing in my backyard and think of how my dad used to push me. If those moments were repeated now, I would not feel the same. I am not the same and neither is he. My dads joyous eyes have been sucked out by life's ordeals and so have mine. You, my darling, have seen my true colors and have grown sick of me. Just as I of you.

The problem with good moments is that they are just that, moments. Moments don't last forever and should not. All that is left is that sweet or sour taste in your tongue. Your heart then has to do some processing, a few things get adjusted and then things are different. You begin to feel lost and then you are. What's there to do, but be nostalgic?

Nostalgia has a weird effect too. I feel like I'm floating in space and looking at my belly. I look down at my belly because it feels strange. I think about how my mother would feed me through my belly button and how she does not anymore. I do not care because I cannot remember. My mother held me in her belly though, does she feel the same emptiness? Does she miss me? I start to wish for love, but reject the thought of wishing for it. Wishing for love distracts me from looking at my belly. I look at my belly because that is where the pain is and I want it to stop. It is annoying.

I know what false hope is and once I give into it my belly begins to hurt more and more. The scariest part is that sometimes I can't do anything about it. I am, after all, floating in space with this pain.

Space: a lonesome and cold place. I feel naked. No one can see me though. If they did, I would not care. What mattered most has disappeared a while back and my body has become nothing. There were times when I could blind my heart with pass times. There were times when I had someone to lay with. There were times when memories were nice. I felt the ground then. It was a feeling though.

I am always floating. I will always float.

It is real and beyond me. Beyond hope.

All I do is wait for anything.

I remember not to dream.

How Warmth is Hell

There's no better way to describe the feeling of a certain moment I am thinking about than the word warmth.

Warmth under the sheets with his body bundled up against hers. Warmth in his heart because there was no better feeling than to lay close to her and smell her natural aroma. Warmth in the room thanks to a small heater that was alone in the corner. Her body was stiff and alert at the screen they both were supposed to be watching. He was looking at her though. He was observing how the screens reflection painted her skin neon blue and how very well it suited her.

All the warmth vanished, however, in a split of a second when she turned around and asked with a hint of a demand "Are you watching? Or do you not care?".

He obviously replied "Your skin is neon blue! I love you".

She ignored the affection and answered with a blunt "You're an asshole".

He replied with a frown.

The warmth then came back, but it was not the same. His skin was sweaty, his ears were boiling and his head felt as if it was about to burst. He soon realized these were the fires of hell, and they hurt him. It was no longer just warm, it was heated. He was heated, both outside and in.

Ever since that day he prefers to watch TV with the heater off. The heater doesn't feel the same to him. It was once a selfless being that attempted to warm those who are in need of comfort. Now it feels like a demon mockingly watching the world burn in a mischievous corner where it controls everything.

The girl, however, still looks good with the screen reflecting on her skin.

However, he begun to watch more the TV and not her.

Nothing as a Remedy

He lays there in his bed watching a TV show he doesn't care for but needs to watch to keep his brain busy.

He's living off nothing to be numb.

He lays there in the party watching the girls pass by and wishes them, but wishes more the drugs to stop wishing.

He's living off nothing to be numb.

He would rather lay there and look at the ceiling without the feeling of motivation, so there is not possible feelings of failure.

He's living off nothing to be numb.

He lays there in his kitchen with food, food that he likes. Is he hungry? No, but it tastes good and that's as good as life gets for him.

He's living off nothing to be numb.

He can't stop wanting and there's nothing more that he wants than to stop wanting.

He's living off nothing to be numb.

A Conversation I Had With Myself

What was that all about?

I don't know. I just saw something nice and I went for it.

I guess that makes sense, but where did the nice something go?

It was there. Till it wasn't. And then I just wasn't.

What?

The good became the bad and the knowing of it became one-sided.

Are you sad?

I wish. I'm not. I'm nothing.

Why are we talking?

I don't know. I think I need help because I feel weird, but I'm not scared. I'm just here.

...

Same.

The unsolvable case.

There has to be a sequel though, right?

I guess all you can do is hope.

That's all I have. If that breaks then I'll have nothing.

Well at least I'm here.

Yeah, but then aren't we just wasting space?

I love you though.

You don't. Love is fake. You just like my company and I like yours. There's nothing anyone can contribute to another except that.

Isn't that enough?

No. Not for me. I'm not satisfied. I don't know if I ever will be.

...

...

So what's the point?

None. I'll just float and see what happens. I'm sure something will spark my interest eventually and give meaning to my life for a moment. It'll be just that though: a moment. It's okay though. I'll pretend I accomplished something, my ambitions will be met and I'll keep on hoping for more.

Live and die for nothing?

That's what its always been, but who's keeping an eye out for it?

Not me.

You shouldn't. No one should, because any fantasy is better than a reality.

What a world...

It's completely random and therefore pointless. You're in that chaos and you become just as insignificant as it. Nothing matters so you just do what you want, to just realize nothing's changed. Nothing will ever change. That's free will for you! Then you die and those who loved you never understand.

That's sad.

Well, at least you get to do what you want. Right? And endless possibilities?

Yeah. But it's still sad.

Just go back to your fantasy...

Cocoon

My head spins faster each day that passes.

My dizzy eyes betray my line of sight.

My stomach is a punching bag for my emotions.

I want to cry, but my mouth is a jail for my cry.

I check the mirror and none of these things are reflected.

Am I so weird?

Wait for Tomorrow

See what you want to see.

This world is how it's meant to be.

Today has been canceled.

Go back to bed.

Everything will reset.

I lied.

Section 5: Conscience

What I think most mammals do not have, except those who consider themselves humans.

A Brains Power

I think my brain is tired of thinking. It has been doing this ever since I was born. It will continue to do so till I die. I don't know if thinking makes you smart, self aware, wiser, anxious, or whatever people tell you. I just know the action and found the best fit word that the dictionary provides. I do not know if imagination can be considered thought.

Thinking can be scary though. Thinking can make me think of horrendous acts that only the most heinous of people will do. I once was 5 and thought about how I could kill. Not that I wanted too, but that I could. And if I could, how?

I became scared and ran to the person whom I thought of stabbing, my own mother. I apologized. She forgave me without any concern.

"It's all in the head", she said. And that's where it stayed.

Thinking can make me think of joyous possibilities that reside in me and hope to project onto reality if allowed too. I was once 15 and thought of myself with ten gorgeous women. We were naked and we had hunger for each other. I did not tell my mother.

My brain provides its own realm for me. This realm is like the wild west, where everything counts. Escapism at its most discreet and powerful form. All in the daylight. Is that a crime?

Now the moon is out and I am tired. I have thought too much. So I must go to sleep and dream. Dreaming is thoughts brother. A main difference is that dreams take my soul and I do not know what happens. I will be put in a threshold more powerful than the realm of thought. I will be lost.

What is the weirdest thing for me is that brains are always working!

They get tired from thinking and recover from dreams?

I Am Normal

Something has to be real because then there would be nothing. We do not know what is real, however, because we each live in our own worlds. Some describe what goes on as science and others as subliminal. Some have more evidence than others. Everyone's life is subjective and there is not a common ground any of us truly have. As real as that is, what does that say about ourselves? That we are all detached from reality? In a very basic way, yes. We are. We all live in our own bubble, but that's fine. The possibility to interpret the world and ourselves in our on way is what gives us a sense of direction. A purpose. The path we take is solely based off this purpose and we utilize the energy within our bodies to fulfill it. Isn't that free will? I believe in that. How I know we have free will is because of the spontaneous things that happen in life. What we all do as collectives causes chain reactions in ways no one can even begin to imagine. Isn't that the Butterfly Effect? It is all like the theory that says that energy is neither created or destroyed. Energy is transferred and we choose how that energy is transferred. If there is a greater someone, it gave us this energy and the power to do as we wish with it. We are our own Gods thanks to science. The world is full of random variables that cannot be controlled and go on forever. Just like the universe. Isn't that infinity? If we all did the same thing and things were predetermined there would be a beginning with an end. Is that what God planned? Energy is recycled for years to come and it will do as it pleases. We carry on the legacy of energy by having it to satisfy our will. This whole notion is how I see the world. It is completely subjective. I am just a vessel caring energy that will be reused by something else. I am nothing and everything at the same time. I can do everything and nothing at the same time. Each is a cure to its own malice. Is that crazy or a paradox? Grey. Black. White.

Subjective Morals

I know how I feel,
but I don't know if what I think is correct.
What is right and wrong is so
relative.

A Martyr is Good?
What's the
hidden pleasure in
sacrifice?

I Need Comfort in You
Why is fear a fight or flight,
but also a fuck and cum?

A Lack of Value Judged Through Different Perspectives
Out of pure oblivion I was not appreciated.
Is doing it intentionally any worse?

We Are Just Human

Don't tell me
forever, because forever is a
sin.

Animals With Big Brains that Make the Animals Think They Are Better

Our brains have not evolved, just our bodies and our phones.

The way we live life is primal in every aspect.

Our brains trick us into believing otherwise.

Maybe that is why we are such a success, but never perfect?

We are mammals.

The word "humans" was invented by people with a superiority complex.

Logistics to Keep Pretending?
It's a fact, so it is what it is.
Accept it or not, ask yourself:
are you still
pretending?

Section 6: Hopeless

When you feel as if there is no point to anything, but you want there to be a point to anything.

This Rain is Comforting

I'm not usually too fond of rain, but lately it seems to calm me.

Rain feels like emotions being expressed onto the earth and I like that.

It grabs what I have stored and puts it out there for me.

I feel better now, since you are my outlet.

There is still a crack in the sky where I see the sun.

It is disappearing.

I am okay with that.

Running for Myself

I wish that what I felt you would see as right because you understand my methods, just like I understand yours. You're too caught up in your own world that you don't see me and if you ever do, you're confused. Without realizing it you've left me alone and it hurts. I keep running to you expecting you at the finish line, but it's hopeless because you're not at the finish line. It's just me running in circles finding myself at the end all alone and where I started. I thought that if I tried to gain better legs to run I would catch you. However, you made me lose the heart that gave me the legs. I should have learned by now it is all so pointless. Sadly, I still run at times when my heart gets oiled up with hope. Maybe I should not run so that I "wish that what I felt you would see as right because you understand my methods, just like I understand yours". Maybe I should just run and be okay with not being understood by you. Yes it is a lonesome run, but my importance should come along with the simple act of just running. So I will run for myself since the only person who is guaranteed to be at the finish line is me. It always was me. I do hope that people cheer my name. They do not have to though.

I Choose Humanity Over Insanity

Okay, so I am writing this because I feel that my head is drifting away.

I am not sure if I will be the same as I was yesterday.

I am changing as time goes by.

Into the abyss that is nothing my soul is trapped and the temptation of freedom feels like an ultimatum.

I do not like what is happening, but the outcome of whatever I am meant to be does not matter in an overarching way.

However, if I see this life through a subjective view I should try and savor whatever is left of my soul.

Although it is all fake, it is nice and I want to keep that much.

So I will not drift into this abyss for the sake of my duality.

Its an unstable, but balanced existence.

If Being Genuine Was Normal
I just want to live
the rest of my life
basing people off first impressions.

You Make You and I Make Me

I will listen to your history,
but do not force me to
care for it.

Money Could be my Friend
Should I get rich
to compensate for this lack of
love?

The Body, the Mind and the Heart

I go to bed every night
trying to figure out how to describe what I
feel, but I can't.
I know what I need
though.

Gasping Either Way

I feel naked without my
mask,
but the mask suffocates
me.

Section 7: Darkness

The not so pleasant side of being human.

The Dark Side

There is a dark part to everyone's soul. This darkness is masked by our oblivious innocence that has been bashed into our brains. We can either learn to coexist with this sinking hole of ours or live blind to the true nature of our being. I am not saying to embrace this darkness, but rather just be aware of its ambition. Free yourself to yourself and then learn to apply what makes you. Coexisting with yourself and what is around. Freedom of thought and expression.

How I Used You

I want to feel you near and for you to understand that I do not want you. I just need certain things and everything will be alright, for me at least. I am my main concern. Now I do not care to say these things, it is just necessary. I do not wish to waste more time explaining myself.

Just give me a nights dose of humane proximity and its warmth that tickles my insides. Give me that sincere satisfaction that comes along when you pride yourself in me, in every way possible. Give me the confidence that comes along with your loyalty. Give me your insanity when I am bored and give me your peace when I am anxious. Be my personal tool, like is my job. Give me purpose.

Do all that, but do not put me in chains. I want freedom of concern in all forms. Because any concern is in it of itself a jail. Give me love without ties.

I shall forever be happy with a connection, but no compromise.

Be my needs to my end.

My life just wants you, but never needs you.

Indifference

The most comfortable feeling is indifference to one's self. I do not hate nor do I love myself. It is strange and for some intolerable. Death and life are equal to me. So what's the point I ask myself?

I live off temptations and the only temptation I have left is to see what this life offers. I hope to not get bored. I hope to find what gives my body a jolt, if there is such a thing out there. I've come to peace with my loneliness and as long as I am entertained, I have fun.

All I am doing is hoping for something better, but I never have any expectations. I don't even know if I am capable of giving myself such a thing as "hope" if it requires faith. Which it does.

I feel as if there's just nothing and then me.

What does one do with nothing, knowing it is just that?

Dream?

Well, I try.

Withdrawal

It's not that I miss you and want you back.

I just want the things I used you for to still be mine.

I want to have a person that I can go to if I want intimacy.

I want my body to touch another's in the same way.

I want to have someone I can snuggle up against on a rainy day and talk to when I'm nervous.

I want that connection, but I do not want the commitment.

I do not want to miss this person.

I do not want to love this person.

I just want to use them and for them to be okay with it.

I want causality over exclusivity.

I want you as a drug.

Break What Matters

Let me just throw back and watch the world spin on its axis.

Let me be a viewer with a passive attitude and no fucks to give.

Let me just do what I want without any repercussion because responsibilities are a bitch.

Let me push forward, without any effort.

I don't care if I win or lose, just the strength alone is enough.

Let me wish and have, rather than wish and wait.

Let me be and, for my own good, stop caring for others.

Let me be everything I want and all I hate, just to chop it up and feed it to peasants.

Let me be my ego, I let you.

An Annoying Day in a Plane

Can the kids in the back shut the fuck up.

Can the grown men in the back stop laughing.

Can the flight attendant stop fucking talking.

I can't fucking stand anyone right now.

I have been trying to read.

I have been trying to sleep.

I can't even listen to my fucking music without someone ruining it.

I can't have a single nice moment.

I'm tired.

Annoyed.

Super fucking anxious.

I was in the bathroom and the toilet kept on flushing by itself.

My ass is wet.

Lights keep on turning off and on.

People keep on talking and drying their hands with machines that make frequencies that bother me.

Im so fucking mad.

It's also cold.

Also my mind keeps on thinking about...

This needs to end.

I remember my means and so I do.

The Eye of the Black Hole

I finally feel fine and its boring.

Having to fight your hearts pain is more engaging than living okay.

Give me pain because I enjoy the chase of leaving it, it is the true high.

I hate coming to the norm, the next extreme of my life is what I seek for.

My ill mind is only for few to understand because it is in another language, making English the best facade.

I keep on falling to pit bottom.

I feel the black hole.

I see what beauty it sucks.

I die with that beauty lingering in my memory.

A Blob

A blob is on my bed. It's plain like a forgotten memory and still like a whiff of death. It smells as if it were rotting away into nothingness and seems to suit it just right. It leaves a moist stain of grease, but it doesn't care. All you see are its eyes that look beaten. You wonder how it got here. You don't know the answer, so you lay next to it. You just accept. It's there when you wake up and there when you go to sleep. You realize it's incomplete, just like you. He's my brother.

The Paradox of Philosophy

I am a man of reason and what I am scared of the most is to do for no reason.

I have tried to find a reason to love myself and I found myself.

I have tried to find a reason to love life and I found freedom.

When I try to give my own reasons to do, I am faced with uncertainty.

What is happiness?

Meh

I haven't felt in a while.

Today I did and it just reminded me of why I stopped in the first place.

True feelings are overwhelming and it's better when things are left unfini

Who Agrees?
So much easier to deal with a
hangover than a
fucking
relationship.

I Am Mature

This is just how
I feel
and my indifference of it
all is
rotten.

I Want Your Addiction
Cry
help like you
need
rehab from
me.

Home, Sweet Home

I'm okay with living in a shitty
world because I feel a part of
it.
I am home.

Loneliness' Sidekick

I hate when there isn't anyone to keep me company
because it forces me to spend
time with me
which makes me realize how much I hate myself.

Being Free Through Freedom of Concern
Happy to be
sick and single
so no one really
has to care about me!

Don't love me,
its too much
pressure.

Love is a toxic feeling
if it involves
others.

The Inverse of Paradise

The end of Never Land
is a pit black void
that makes you a part of its emptiness.

Laziness' Sidekick
Only trying
when things
feel wrong.

Section 8: Lightness

The not so pleasant side of being God.

Recovery

This is just how I feel and the indifference of it all is rotten. The lack of motivation I have feeds the vermin within me. I need a jolt of electricity to either end me or move me. I don't care, as long as this feeling goes away. To relish upon my apathy is not something to be glorified, but rather loathed. However, it is a vice. A vice so dishonorable that I shall be executed by the same muscles that I caused so much pain to: my hearts desires. Only then will my death have any sort of justifiable means to an end. I am a walking paradoxical human mind, with a pure heart and rusty old arms. Nothing but a bromide afflicted by sheer laziness. Do I know love? All I know is me. Success can only be measured by oneself and I see nothing. My life is full of self inflicted forgettable actions, and like them, I am forgotten. I am living off toxic gas that burns my lungs which incinerates my heart. It helps as an illusion. I am alone and like a coward am seeking refuge. In other words, imma fucking pussy. Where did my courage go? I feel drugged and find it okay, which is what I despise the most. By Monday I shall hope to be a new man, if not I am only seconds away from doom.

Am I Transcending?

There are three kinds of people in this world.

Those who are born to live up to ideals and are okay with it.

Those who do not care for ideals and are okay with it.

And those who do not care for ideals and are not okay with it.

These three people can also be divided by three categories of existence.

Those who live in essence.

Those who live in presence.

And those who struggle with a certain transition.

The Power of Imagination

If you wake up from a nice dream and choose to be upset about the fact that it was "just a dream" and it was not real, that's because you're letting your ego get the best of you.

The feelings of any dream are just as real as if the dream became true.

Being able to fantasize is a noble endeavor and even nobler if it lets you achieve your fantasy.

Puzzles

Someone today told me I was freedom. I appreciate the compliment, but as my profound self likes to ruin anything good, I did not like the statement. In this world, there is the chaos we face when we see that a perfectly good person can be unreadable due to a mental illness. You look into their eyes and see that there's nothing there. That untamable void is what freedom is.

A bird can only fly when it chooses too. It can choose not to, it can die and it can break its wings. If you find comfort in the idea of flying then by all means fly, but do not call that freedom. Know that it is not the chaos that will let you fly, but your will power to take on the chaos. Flying is freedom, but heights is something one must take on. Can You?

I cannot be freedom, I am simply in it. I just choose to do whatever. Am I choosing right? What is choosing right?

What I did to seek this answer is that I went back in my head and looked at times when America was truly free. I read books of the roaring 20s and stories about the wild west. This was when all men were at an even playing field. No rules and Darwinism took its toll on humanity.

So who were the ones that were on top?

If Darwin's theory is at all accurate, we are at a primitive level animals and what puts us on top is the brain. It is proven already by how we are the smartest mammal and clearly the most dominant. So as an animal the ones that reach the top are the ones who I should idealize. Right? Yes, to some extent.

I do believe that we should admire the Rockefellers and the confidence artist of the 20s. They were savvy and prospered as a result. Kings. To another extent I see the cowboys that saved towns just as honorable. They may not of been too savvy, but they were full of drive and the heart of the town they were. Heroes.

How did these people not face the anguish of freedom? Freedom is the nothingness of the universe.

The only way I can wrap my head around all of this is by saying that the universe created us in such a way that made mammals want success in a tyrant, yet heroic fashion. These motifs are universal through cultures. The cool guy and the nice guy? How do we become gods and kings? Isn't that a pretentious question? Do we all have a superiority complex we are unaware of? I think we do. Is there something else to this? I know a god is to holy for us and a tyrant too controlling. Most of us choose to shoot for the stars. Is there something wrong with that? What's the in between for our lovely patrons of the earth?

Maybe the answer is not out there. It is in us and it always has been. Gods and Kings, are all concepts we created. They're just as fake as they are real. Yeah batman doesn't fucking exist, but I do and the person who created him does too. When I read batman when I was young, I would dream that batman was my dad. Maybe batman was the creator's dad too? I doubt it. I do bet that, just like my dad, the creator's dad was himself and whatever feeling my dad gave me is a universal feeling and this feeling is subjective for everyone. We are our own idols. Don't you see? Believe in yourself.

I never was religious nor did I understand tyranny. I just understood the feelings and I am sure many others did too.

I guess what I am trying to say is that like a puzzle we are alike in the sense that we are puzzle pieces. However, we are scattered and we do not know where we belong.

We are all alike in some way, but the chaos of the universe scatters us everywhere and all we can do is try to solve this puzzle which we call life.

I believe that to solve this puzzle, you have to know what piece you are and which ones match with you.

Please explore, but also take steps back to reflect.

And never forget that no puzzle piece is the same.

When I hold your hand, I feel something bigger.

Do not Let me taint your part in this crazy puzzle.

Stay objectively subjective and subjectively objective!

Universal Laws

A hero
somewhere
is a hero
everywhere.

Symmetry is
math and a
feeling.

We have nothing,
but free will makes
us create everything.

If you are to depend on
someone or something,
that better be the thing
you love
most.

The Use of Love

I've loved you and that made me the best kind of person for you.
Now I love myself and am the best kind of person for myself.

To Those I Love
I spare you the suffering,
you are too nice to tell me
what you truly feel.
Now we both live a performance, but we know.
Is that okay?

Section 9: Inanimate

The unknown that I am not questioning.

My Duality Is Like Yours

A tendency to escape reality when it starts to hurt.

The power to fog up memories that broke me.

Lying to myself as much as possible to feel serenity.

All I learn is that as much as I try to run from the pain it always waits for me at the finish line.

It waits patiently to ultimately sneak up into my brain and strip me of my subconscious demons.

It reaches into my thoughts, exposing what I held in the dark for so long.

I now see what I have been blind to for so long, Im aching.

I despise confronting myself, but I know I must, for I am drowning.

Mirror break.

Self reflection disappear.

Yes I feel naked without my mask, but the mask suffocates me.

It's a paradoxical situation and juxtapositions suck.

Worth

He was perfection.
So he was challenged for everything.
He fought with everything and beat nothing.
He was perfection.
So he was challenged for his mind.
He fought with his mind and beat the body.
He was perfection.
So he was challenged for his body.
He fought with his body and beat the mind.
Now he is perfection.
What shall he do?

Private Soul

This wall blocks the
noise and it is very
nice.
I can talk to myself better like
this.
I am a huge fan of
intimacy.

What is "Real Life"?

I hate looking at the mirror because it shows
me
that I am here and living.
That reality scares me,
I want this to be a
dream.

How this All Works

I am
gullible,
but I
know.

Section 10: Power
What we all have, but should never want.

A Wise Old Man

Fear powers the house of respect,
like my father.
Devotion powers the house of love,
like my mother.
Tranquility powers the house of peace,
like my freedom.

Stopped In Place

Petrified lonesome soul.

Could you not feel the cold.

I am here for comfort.

Do not taste the dirt.

Shoes put on backwards.

What am I walking towards?

I am confused.

I am scared.

I need your hand.

Faith

I believe in what you said, therefore I believe in you.

I believe in what I do in accordance to you.

I believe in what I stand for, do you believe in me?

Because I am frightened by you, even though I love you.

Punctuation on the No

I stand here waiting for your approval, but
I see nothing in sight.
I stand here with my legs shaking, but
I know this is not what you want.
I stand here hoping for your will, but
I know I came too late.
Now I stand alone, alone in this rain.

Reputation at its Finest to Ask for Death

I yawn.

I stare.

My eyes are watery, but feel dry.

I sweat.

I jitter.

My hand clasp to each other.

I wonder.

I say.

Nothing concrete comes out, but noise.

Stuttered Once Upon A Time

I had difficulty with the basics, but I found strength
in my fundamentals at birth.
I had difficulty with the scream for aid, but I found strength
in my souls yearning.
I had difficulty with the will of God, but I found strength
in my moralities.
Do you approve of what is left?
Do you approve what I left?

Institutionalized
Thank you for your duties as a
community,
but fuck you for your
pressure.

Ending

Heavenly Father,

I think what I feel.

I feel what I live.

I do what I believe.

I believe in this.

I will always appreciate this.

I hope you can agree.

In Jesus name amen.

Conclusion to my *stuff*:

Thank you for your time!

If you have anything lingering in your head after all of this *stuff*, just know there is a method.

I appreciate this.

I hope my dreams came true.

Made in the USA
Middletown, DE
07 March 2019